STORY OF A CRAZY GIRL- THE SECRET PET

AARNA GUPTA

Made with ♥ on the Notion Press Platform
www.notionpress.com

To my Father

to whom I shall remain indebted

for setting the foundation

on which this book is based

Contents

Foreword

Preface

I am a young amateur writer of 10 years old and really excited about this story.

This is a story of a little girl who loves to have pets, let's see what will happen!!! will she be able to fulfil her dream or it will remain a dream only!!!!!

Acknowledgements

Any accomplishment requires the effort of many people and this work is no different. I thank my brother and especially my father, whose encoouragement and assistance was instrumental in accomplishing this task. I wish to express my gratitude to Creative Era, Anurag, Aryan who helped me in laying the stepping stone for me for writing books. Their motivation, guidance helped me a lot. I thank Notion Press for giving me an opportunity to publish my book and giving all support to new budding writers.

ONE

Hi, this is a story of a crazy girl. This is not my first book, it is my second good but it is a series by me, Aarna Gupta. Let me introduce myself, I am Aarna, worlds naughtiest, funniest and craziest girl.

You will not believe that in this story I have revealed you a big secret. So, let's begin the story.

One evening on my street I saw one cat with her little kittens. I was drawn to the kittens. They were so small, soft and were all cuddled to their mother. I felt a strong pang to hold them in my hands but left them to enjoy their mother love. Although I left from there, I kept on thinking about them.

I tried many times but was not able to trace them again. After few days, I was going to the market to buy graph copy for summer holidays HW when suddenly my wallet dropped. When I bent down to pick it up, I noticed something was moving near the bush. I went near it and was astonished to see one small little kitten was lying in our society garden.

I tried to pick it up in my hands but she seemed to be very sacred. I placed it again on the ground and searched for her mother and other kittens. I could not find any of them, then I called my friend Kaavya. We again tried searching for her mother but were not successful.

Kaavya said, "May be cat along with her other kittens had shifted to some another place and by mistake one kitten is left". We both decided to take care of the kitten until her mother came and she is reunited with other siblings. Kaavya brought some milk from her home, kitten hurriedly drank and then walked a little bit. We were so happy to see her walking. We searched nearby societies also but could not trace her mother. Now only way to save her little life was to adopt the kitten.

I am a big lover of cats and was VERY eager to have her as my pet. I named my sweetest, cutest pet as "SHITSHI". It is a unique name with no meaning but seeing that cute bundle of joy, this word "Shitshi" only came into my mind. Before taking her to my home as my dearest pet there was a big problem, I had to take my parents' permission.

With glitters in my eyes and butterflies in stomach I danced towards my house. Mom was watering the plants she was singing an old song. I thought she seems to be in good mood and will definitely agree, I immediately blurted out that I saw a small kitten nearby. Just listening to this, she raised her eyebrows and took me to task. I couldn't even reply back to her, forget about requesting her and nice things I had thought I would share with my mother about the kitten.

With a long face and moist eyes, I returned to the playground. I had forgotten everything about my holiday HW. I don't want to see her die, with hook or crook I just wanted to save her precious life.

I ran towards uncle Raman house to get some planks of wood. I was pretty sure that he will definitely be having some because there was repair work going in his house. Uncle Raman has a heart of gold, always ready to help others. When I told about Shitshi, he readily not only provided me with wood but told me that if required he will send his carpenter also to help me.

I got wooden planks and ran towards Banyan tree. Meanwhile Kavya arranged ladder from security guard and placed it near the tree.

After 4 hours of toiling, we made it something like a nice place to live for Shitshi with floor from the branches of the tree and just keep my pet away from dangers. Although it seemed to be safe from all the angles we can think off, I was little afraid what will happen if someone will complain about my beloved Shitshi to security. My another big concern was who we be able to manage to provide her food at regular intervals as my mother had already told me to forget about her and concentrate on my upcoming unit tests which were scheduled immediately after my holidays.

I was determined not to lose hope and try my level best. Some other friends also joined hands and all of us tried to keep her supply of milk always overflowing. For some days I just took my glass of milk and few biscuits from cupboard and went to the tree and give it to my Shitshi.

For some days my plan went conveniently but one day my Mom was having a doubt as I always use to make faces whenever my mother gives me milk but she was wondering why now a days I always have a smile on my face whenever my mother gave me a glass of milk.

I told her in class we are studying "Food and Health" chapter in science and our teacher enlighten us about importance of nutrients and diseases caused by their deficiency. So now I am cautious about my health. Mom was impressed!!!!

I was elated, everything was going on smoothly and our darling kitten was growing slowly. BUT one day my brother noticed me that as soon as mother served us breakfast, I just vanished from there. He called me and hearing his voice I straight away rushed to table. He asked, "Where did you went? Do you want us to miss the bus? "I said, "Mr. I had gone to see my plants."

I just hate my brother. Every time he keeps on scolding me, sometimes he even hits me when I don't listen to him. Although things were different when I was small. At that time, he used to love me a lot. I have seen in pictures, in hospital when I was born he was sitting beside my mother holding me in his lap with a proud smile on his face, as if I am his prized trophy!!

I think in every sister and brother relationship, when they are in school love is left only 10 %. They just keep on fighting at a drop of hat, fault finding and complaining about each other becomes their all-time favourite time pass. I also do the same to distract my mother from teaching.

But once any one of them goes for graduation then they start missing each other. Oh! I am sorry I started dreaming about time when my brother takes admission in college and sweet bond between us will blossom again. We both took our school bags and rushed towards bus stop to catch the bus.

The bowl in which we feed Shitshi had become too filthy. So, in evening I was looking for some nice bowl for her. I went in kitchen searching for a bowl but dared not to touch any of my mother's crockery because my Mom goes all nuts and will kill me even if she is not able to trace out even a single spoon.

Then I went towards the store room to explore something pleasant but was disappointed to find out that it was locked. I thought hard but could not found any way out so eventually I went to my brother, Sam for help.

I asked Sam, "If I give you $1, will you arrange store key for me?"

He said, "You need store key, Hmm.... for what???? Anyway, I don't care about it but if you give me $2 I will think about it. It is very dangerous and effort required is not worth $1."

I asked, "Ok, you need two dollars. It is too much you are asking for but today I don't have any option". I went to my room and opened my piggy bank. I just shook it hard because I don't want to break it and got $10. I went to Mom and requested her to give me change. She gave me change. I said thanks and rushed to Sam. I gave $2 to Sam and told him to right away open the store room.

Sam said, "I only have to arrange for the store key but in case you want it to get opened also then you have to shed 2 more dollars".

I said, "You just have to arrange me the keys rest I will manage, Thanks for your kind concern".

I was following him then he said to Mom that her parcel came. Mom was surprised. Mom went to the door and in the meantime, he went to mothers' room and took out store keys and gave it to me. I handed him my hard earned two dollars.

The key seemed to be old and there was rust all over. I tried to open the door but it was not working. I again went to Sam and requested him to help me out.

He told me to give two more dollars. I said, "OK. I will tell Mom that you ask for money every time I approach you for some help". He said, "OK, don't tell Mom. I will help you."

Sam tried to open the lock, luckily it opened. But as he tried to enter the door, something strange happened. A loud creak noise came. Hearing the sound, Mom shouted from her room, "What happened???"

Sam whispered don't bother about Mom, you go fast inside the garage and bring me an oil bottle and torch. I rushed to the garage, father saw me. Dad said, "Where are you going?"

I said, "Just going outside in the lawn".

I ran towards the garage. Grabbed torch and oil can and hurried in the direction of store but in a dash hit father on the way. Before he asked anything, I blurted out that tap of bathroom is not working properly, it is covered with rust so I am going there...

Dad was about to say something but without waiting about his reaction I ran.

But then I saw Dad went upstairs. I followed him. Dad saw Sam near the store room. He asked, "What are you doing here? Both of you are not allowed here."

I said, "But Why??"

Dad Said, "There is so much dust and germs, old broken things are lying here and there and you both can get hurt. "

He also warned us about some old crockery kept there which we can break and advised again to stay away. After that, Dad went to his room. Eventually we both had a sigh of relief.

We both went to Sam's room. His room is on ground floor near dining room. It has its own advantages and disadvantages.

Whenever we came back tired from shopping and don't want to climb stairs, we all rest in his room but most of the time when Sam has his exams along with exams always came some guests and neither he is able to study or sleep because of too much noise. He gets irritated a lot.

At night, I went to Sam's room and said, "Hey, Wake up!!"

Sam said, "Who is there??"

I said, "Come to store room".

He said, "Let's go".

We silently went to the store room. I was already carrying the oil bottle.

He took hold of oil bottle from my hand and wiped the lock. He poured some oil on the key and lock. We both waited for few minutes. He tried and with little effort was able to open the door.

Sam kept standing near the door, I raced inside. I was not able to see clearly; some dust too entered my left eye. I rubbed my eye but kept on walking and looking for my precious bowl from one eye.

Just then I banged one big cartoon. Something from inside just told me that I was looking for this cartoon only.

I stealthily opened it and saw beautiful crockery packed inside. I carefully unpacked it. My eyes glistened with joy when eventually I got I was looking for.

I was not able to lift my eyes off from that beautiful bowl.

I got hold of it, admired it to my heart's content and then rearranged all the crockery back.

Holding the priced possession in my hand I rushed toward the door. Sam was waiting for me there. I showed it to him but he was least interested in it.

He locked the door and we went to my room.

I just gave him three Dollars. He was elated to have three dollars and humming his favourite song he went to his room.

I kept the bowl on my study table and went inside the kitchen to fetch some milk.

I wanted to arrange for milk now itself as in the morning, Mom will be in the kitchen and I won't be able to take out milk. I was thinking that in morning what will happen when I will go to my Shitshi and give her milk.

I was visualizing her drinking milk, her content face. How happy she will feel seeing me, her new milk bowl. I was wondering what will make her most happy, milk, myself or new glittering bowl.

In the morning I told Mom that I am going in garden for watering plants and went to my dearest pet. Shitshi was elated to see me and immediately slurped the milk. I was pleased to see her and happily went to school.

In school I was not able to concentrate in my class, my mind was wandering what Shitshi would be doing now. I told Kaavya how I was able to arrange bowl for her. She too felt happy for Shitshi.

I was thinking about my pet, when Ma'am tapped my head, "Hey Aarna, where are you looking??? Pay attention to your book."

My teacher is very pretty but she is nice only look wise actually she is very cruel. Her name is Vicky, Miss Vicky. She only appreciates students who flatter her.

She always appreciates those students who keeps on buttering her. She is a teacher of maths and as you know getting good grade in maths is a herculean task and for me it is next to impossible.

Let me tell you something about my classmates, a nerd girl name Jessica and a very straightforward girl Rose.

Jessica never leaves a chance to flatter Miss Vicky like, today you are looking very nice, Wow! what a great explanation, since yesterday I was trying to understand this topic, nobody can make maths so easy. We are so lucky to have a teacher like you... and list goes on and on....

In class test, Rose got 19/20 and Jessica got 14 out of 20 but Miss Vicky appreciated Jessica in front of whole class and didn't said even a single nice thing or appreciated Rose efforts.

Rose felt bad but as always, she did not say anything. This is a cheating but Miss Vicky and Jessica are OMG!!!

Today in the class also same type of thing happened. In the class we got Maths assessment which was very difficult. Vicky Ma'am said, "If you have any doubt, please raise your hand."

I was having doubt in question 10. I asked her to please clarify but she said, "Sorry this question is very very easy, please try yourself."

I felt very bad. This is not a correct way to treat your students. After a short while, nerd Jessica asked Ma'am for same question number 10 and then she went to the board and explained very nicely to her.

After I reached home, I came to know that my mother's sister and her family are coming for dinner. She loves me a lot and always bring something special for me. Every one was so happy, mummy was busy preparing delicacies for dinner and told me to keep the dinner table ready. She told papa to bring grocery set from store. Hearing this my colour faded.

Father brought crockery cartoon from the store room and kept it into kitchen. Mumma started taking it out for cleaning. I was petrified, then only mumma said, "I am not finding one bowl, it is missing. It is my favourite dinner set. I have carefully packed it, where it might have gone???"

My heart skipped a beat.

Grandma said, no one went in store and store room is always locked. It must be in the box only.

Hearing this, Dad stared at me. He said, "There was oil on store lock, Aarna yesterday you were carrying oil bottle and torch??? Have you spilled some oil on the lock?"

I stammered, "I...I.... I don't know. I don't know anything..."

That crockery set is very precious to Mom. I glanced at her. Her eyes were full of tears, she was just holding her tears.

I couldn't keep mum now. I started crying and hugged Mom. All were staring at me, all of sudden what has happened to me??

Sorry Mom, very very sorry. I have taken your bowl. Actually actually, I want to feed my little kitten.

I was terrified as I thought my mother would scold me or worse, make me get rid of my secret pet. But to my surprise, my mother was understanding.

I hugged her and told everything about Shitshi. She too hugged me and asked, "Where is your Shitshi??? Will you not show it to me?"

I couldn't believe my ears but my happiness knew no bounds and I joyfully jumped to bring my sweet pet to her new sweet home.

From that day on, I was no longer the crazy girl with just one secret. I had another one – Shitshi. But this time, I was happy to keep this secret. I was so happy to have Shitshi with me. We spent all our time together. I would take her for walks, play with her and even talk to her. Shitshi was no longer just a pet, she was my best friend.

As Shitshi grew up, she became more and more playful. I loved playing with her, but sometimes I would get tired. That's when Kaavya and my other friends would step in to help me. We all loved Shitshi and we all took care of her.

Printed by Libri Plureos GmbH in Hamburg,
Germany